HE/SHE SMELLS A HOO-HOO

He/She Smells a Hoo-Hoo

An Elegant Epic

By
Jack Bunbury

MacDonald Warne Media

Published by MacDonald Warne Media

ISBN: 978-0-9939183-6-0

Cover art by Achraf Amiri
Cover and page layout by Dianna Little

Visit us at:
macdonaldwarnemedia.com
achrafamiri.com

For Sassy, Netta and Nora

On the 15th of June, in the Jungle of Jools,
in the heat of her hotness, in the Pool of the Cool,
she was splashing… in a vintage two-piece pastel
when He/She the Elegant smelled a small smell.

So He/She stopped splashing. She checked her waxed pits.
That's funny, she thought. *I must be losing my wits.*
Then she smelled it again! Just a very faint scent
rudely shrinking her violets without her consent.

I must stop it, thought He/She. *But what is it? Where?*
She prodded and she poked but could feel nothing there
but those small specks of reek floating past through the air.
"I say!" muttered He/She. "I've never heard tell
of an odor so vile, it shrank nippies as well.

"So you know what I think? Why, I think that there is
some mystery befouling my mango rum fizz.
Some dreadful confoundment, something Oh-So-Not-Cool
spritzing and spurting and letting loose in my pool.

"… oh, poor little me, I'm just aquiver with fear
that my bombshell bouffant is now smelling so queer.
I'll just have to fix it, 'cause, between me and you,
He/She don't do dos dabbed with dinky do-do."

So, gently and using the utmost of care,
the Elegant paddled her way to the stair.
She debarked her inflatable chaise longue with grace
and dried her best features—and the ones on her face.

"Hump!" humped a voice. 'Twas a wee pekepoo.
And the pekepoo at his pouch said "Hump!" too.
"Why, that scent is as thin as your peach negligee.
Find the source of that stink? There is no earthly way!"

"Believe me," said He/She, stepping out of the sun,
"my nose is quite keen, though it's had some work done.
This god-awful odor is ruining my hair.
It is choking my throat like a ca-ca éclair."

"I think you're a fool!" laughed the wee pekepoo
and the pekepoo at his pouch said, "Hump two!"
"You're just a big fool in your Jungle of Jools!"
And the pekepoos lapped at the Pool of the Cool.

"You must stop all that lapping!" He/She declared,
"We don't know what foul foulness has landed in there.
I've got to protect you. I'm bigger than you."
So she picked up poo one and got a bag poo too.

Then He/She minced in to her Bungalow Chateau
(which was Spanish Revival, for those in the know).
She powdered her bits and refloofed her hair
and spent twenty-nine minutes on what not to wear.

Finally, she settled on a lace bustier,
a little buff number like a lemon parfait.
She found a travelling skirt so cute that she squealed
and some sensible shoes that were champagne flute-heeled.

The next hour zipped by, finding outfits for poos
and doing their nails so they went with her shoes.
But at last, after soaps and their afternoon quiche
they made a grand exit, both the leashed and unleashed.

Once outside her jooled walls, past the gate, on the street
He/She sniffed through the smog and exhaust and the heat.
"It seems to be reeking from north, south, west and east
like the pilled hairy crack of some large sweaty beast."

"Oh, pshee and pshaw!" said her first pekepup.
"Yeah! Pshaw!" humped the other, now getting worked up.
"The finding of smells, why, at that we're the best—
if you don't count looking cute or snapping at guests.

"Just follow us west down the boulevards and streets.
We'll lead you to that smell, as long as you brought treats."
So with one final pat of her snack pack and rack,
the trio were launched, there was no looking back.

Each garden that they passed received critiques from all,
shrewd observations and of course, warm pee on walls.
At the place with six cats came a sharp bark or two
and some low growls at the house with one cockatoo.

By early evening, home was quite far away.
Her usual walk was now more slog than sashay.
"Hurry up!" snapped her pupkins, "We're barely halfway!"
But He/She had never had this much exercise
since using real chicken in her chicken puff pies.

With each foot on her feet, with each yard, every inch
her shoes, while quite gorgeous, were beginning to pinch.
Her delicate girl toes, after seventeen blocks
were feeling more male than any post office box.

Then just as they turned onto a busy main drag
some very unbuff buffoon pulled up in his Jag.
He had icky brown hair parted far to one side.
"Hey, Honey," he drooled. "Can I give you a ride?"

He/She stopped where she was and stared straight ahead.
She could be mean, she thought, but decided instead
to deflect with decorum, and turning, she said,
"You're kind, but no thanks, I'm just out with my poodles,
So goodbye, sayonara, fuck off and toodles."

But the poor man persisted, "Hey, cutie!" he called.
"Life is short, don't you know. Let's go have a ball!"
In the movie of this, thought our girl, *the next scene
is me telling the police I was low on caffeine.*

Before any more badness transpired on that block,
a new person appeared and gave He/She a shock.
He was dark-haired and tall, a big strapping young man.
Too bad his fourth finger was sporting a band.

His muscly shirt bore an Italian flag
and under one arm he had a box in a bag.
Perhaps the boy had just come from buying new shoes,
which happened to He/She just reading reviews.

"What's going on here?" he said, approaching the car,
"Leave this nice person alone, whoever you are.
Go on, get lost. What are you, some kind of pervert?
Just keep driving, bud, unless you want to get hurt."

The jerk in the Jag talked back, yelled and swore
till the Ital young man put a dent in his door
the shape and the size of a Prada suede loafer,
which won He/She under and sideways and over.

As the Jaguar sped off, the boy turned to our gal,
who was dreaming of lunch in a distant locale
(a small bit of salad on a Venice canal).
"I'm so sorry," he said, "on behalf of our sex.
I'm not usually violent, it was just a reflex."

But He/She was busy trying hard not to see
that her leashes were starting to wrap 'round his knees.
"My name is Ennio," he said, with a flick of his hair,
which of course was in slo-mo and quite debonair.

"My wife's waiting for me, just a mile up the block
And if you're going that way, you don't have to walk."
"And my pups?" asked He/She, not wanting to assume.
"No problem," said the lad, "there is all kinds of room."

He/She batted her lashes. "My goodness, how nice
that you'd do all this helping, without thinking twice."
All the time she was saddened; her hopes were quite dim
of getting him home and having helpings of him.

The lad's blue sedan was just a few steps away.
He held open her door like some valiant valet.
What could go wrong? He/She wondered, looking inside.
You cannot live your whole life with trust cast aside.

She had to think of her toes, her pups and that reek
which was turning her pool into cess, as we speak.
In the end she scooched in with K-9 and -10
and watched him walk 'round, thanking the butt-gods for men.

"This will not end well," muttered one pekepoo,
and the other mini-mutt muttered, "Too true!"
"It might end in some dungeon, you tied up with rope!"
"Hush!" said He/She, with a bustier boost. "Let's hope."

Once the lad was inside with his shoes and his keys,
our girl felt in her tummy a curious unease.
It rose up by itself, this strange bit of doubt
and it flashed through her mind: she might have to get out!

But before she could rethink or cause a delay
the sedan left the curb and was speeding away.
Thankfully, the Italian calmed her a bit
with good-natured chatter that just wouldn't quit.

He had a mole on his calf. His wife never drank.
His two singing budgies were named Dino and Frank.
He couldn't watch soccer since his team lost the cup.
Oh, goodness, thought He/She, *will you ever shut up?*

After ten full minutes of this runaway horse
something snagged the stallion and veered him off course.
"Oh, no!" he said suddenly, bringing He/She's mind back
from going to get cocktails, a gun and a snack.

He was squinting up the block at some youngish thing
in shades, heels and sweats and a great glinting ring.
She was holding her hand just to flash the big stone,
gesturing in Latin as she yelled at her phone.

"She's early," said this formerly big macho dude.
"And I can tell from here she's in one of her moods.
She's sometimes a bit crazy, or jealous, you know,
especially before dinner when her blood sugar's low."

Oh great, thought our He/She, with a sudden regret
that before he got married the boy didn't check
to see if his bride had any bolts in her neck.
"Just stay here," he said, stopping and cracking his door.
"I just need to explain that we've not met before.

"Don't worry," he added, his foot testing the street,
though it was plain, his testes were in full retreat.
Then faking a brave face, he got out, making sure
all the doors of the car were locked tight and secure.

"Oh, look," observed pup one. "Someone's in a fix."
"Fix what?" said pup two, hiding his wee bag of tricks.
"You should have listened to us and not followed that urge.
Now we're all going to end up as skinny bitch purge."

"Have some hope," said He/She, staring out at the walk,
fearing a future with someone's outline in chalk.
For no matter what he said, his hand up to swear,
that Ital young man hadn't the ghost of a prayer.

The very second his wife caught sight of our doll,
she went quiet, her eyes narrowed, but worst of all,
she came at the sedan with a fist full of phone
and smashed at the window till it dialed its last tone.

"Get out of there, whore!" yelled the uncuckolded half
of this duo so batty it made He/She laugh.
"Get out and face me! I'll tear the meat from your bones!"
said this woman who clearly had all her man's stones.

She swore in Italian and English and Czech
with tendons all twerking in her sickly thin neck.
Then with a shard of her phone held up like a knife
she turned to end Ennio, his tight-end and life.

"It's time," offered He/She, "—I think there's no doubt—
we bid bat guano bye-bye and get the hell out."
Unlocking her door, she got one shoe on the street
before Psycho approached, flinging tongue, fists and feet.

At first there was havoc, and a gathering crowd,
with the pekepoos barking unspeakably loud.
But when He/She rose up to her six foot four height
there was a pause—and the banshee's red eyes went white.

Into that pause jumped the husband, loafers and all,
trying vainly to stop an attack on our doll,
for one second later he was cut from the scene
like a case of the runs from a can-can routine.

There's still hope, thought He/She, thinking she could explain
before someone's red blood was circling the drain.
But when she opened her mouth to tell the whole truth
a fast fist with a diamond met slow lip and tooth.

Our girl stepped away with her face full of shock
that all that lipstick and gloss was now all for naught.
And the moment she turned the whack-job attacked,
pulling hard on her hair till she heard her back crack.

The next thing she knew she was flat out on the walk,
surrounded by people who'd just come to gawk.
Disengaging her puppies from her face buffet,
she saw Ennio and freako driving away.

She got to her feet as the crowd quickly dispersed
and not one soul tried helping, which made it all worse.
With one shaking hand she checked her teeth and sore lip
and with the other the bruise that once was a hip.

"Well, this little adventure," said one of her pups,
"has turned into some kind of suckage deluxe."
The other pup rolled his eyes. "We told you so!
Don't pretend for a minute that you didn't know."

"Oh, shish-shush and be quiet," said He/She to them.
"It was just a small error in judgement back then.
I was swayed by the suave, I was piqued by the chic.
Let's get back on the trail of that pool-wrecking reek."

He/She gathered her leashes, and pushed her hair straight
(maybe not straight, but in a more do than done state).
Chin high, gut in, she gave the Hi-Ho! to proceed
on the next part of their trip, mutts sniffing the lead.

The streetlights were lighting, it was rush hour's end
and if they were home and comfy they'd likely spend
time with hors d'oeuvres and TV and maybe a friend.
The stark evening sun at the far edge of the town
had just unzipped the sky and finally gone down.

With her dogkins out front, they marched bravely on
through Little Italy, France and Little Taiwan.
"I'm hungry," said a pup-dog. "It's getting quite late."
"And I have to pee," said the other one. "Oh, wait…"

They'd air-kissed home goodbye what seemed ages ago
and were approaching a place that was almost skid row.
There were peep shows and pawnshops and old greasy spoons
and toothless men staring from their bare-looking rooms.

Several of the houses had young men outside,
smoking some stuff that made them criss- and cross-eyed.
The ones who were awake tried to mutter crude jokes
that were all dribbling drivel to regular folks.

She passed girls of the night who were just waking up
and some kid playing bongos who barked back at her pups.
Then just as they came up to this fried chicken place,
they had to pass a big man with more fat than face.

His rump was supported by two metal chairs
and though she tried not to look, her doggies just stared.
He had two buckets of chicken—or rather, pails
which in retail they referred to as, ew…gross sales.

But the thing that struck even the pupa-mutts dumb
was his open-mouth chawing and great greasy gums.
"Quit staring," hissed He/She. "You must try to be kind."
"He has food!" said one pup. "Are you out of your mind?"

They got by without a prize, which some thought was cruel,
considering their output of blue-ribbon drool.
But before they'd gone past more than nine or ten feet
an old purple car slammed to a stop on the street.

The man who was driving looked whacked-out on drugs.
I'm pretty sure, thought He/She, *he's not here for hugs.*
He had a loud silk shirt with a chest hair bouquet
and was pimped with a cane like a walking cliché.

"What are you doing?" he grumped, his grump voice quite low.
"You can't walk this here corner unless I say so."
He had jumped from his car, which had big rusted fins,
slashing with his cane like a crazed Errol Flynn.

He/She'd barely turned 'round to face this weird guy
before his silver-capped cane was whipping her thighs.
There was no second thought. He/She grabbed at the cane
and shoved it away, then she shoved it again.

"What's wrong with you, sir? Are you totally nuts?
I'm just out for a walk with my two little mutts."
Her pups barked so madly, all chicken-deprived,
they would have settled for eating this loony alive.

At this, the limp pimp came completely undone
and tried to golf both dogs into two holes-in-one.
Seeing the hazard, the mutts ran under his car,
saving their wee skulls from being two under par.

As the pimp turned to He/She, his pimp cane erect,
our girl quickly grabbed it, with a cute sound-effect.
"Na!" she said, with a kicked heel, and then launched the cane
just like any queen launching a ship with champagne.

Well, as bad luck would have it, the cane went askew
and hit fat tubalino mid-chick-chawing chew.
He gave a strange cough and reached for his throat.
That's when panic set in. He was starting to choke!

He/She wanted to help, but was viciously attacked
when the squish-worthy pimple jumped up on her back.
How horrible, she thought as he scratched at her chest;
she'd never had anyone on her so poorly dressed.

"Get off my block," he raged, sticking to her like glue
as she noticed with alarm the whale turning blue.
I've got to hurry, she thought, *or someone might die!*
And I'll be really quite ticked if that someone is I.

Then suddenly remembering from ages past
a quick wrestling trick from her high school gym class
(not the one with the top hat and jock strap, alas),
she dropped herself backward—right on top of the brute,
rendering him unconscious but no less hirsute.

She raced to the man with the bone in his throat
(thinking she'd touch a ten-foot pole, but not that joke).
He had tipped off his chairs, was spazzing on the ground,
with no other person within a hundred yards 'round.

Our He/She got down and pried his greasy mouth wide.
By the glow of the streetlight, she looked deep inside.
Was there a stray bone? A piece of Rhode Island Red?
I'll never forgive myself if he ends up dead!

"Give him the Heimlich!" a pup said, fetching the stick.
"I'm not licking that!" she said, "I'll make myself sick!"
"No, no," said the other pup, "squish up on his guts.
It'll be funny to watch and he might cough up!"

So she got her arms under the man's sweaty pits,
thinking any moment she'd have to call it quits.
The man was so big she had to hug his fat neck
and clutch under his moobs for the proper effect.

She squeezed and she heaved with every ounce of her might
there, in the icky glow of the chicken shack's light.
The pimp had recovered, seen the dog with his cane
and was staggering over, revenge on his brain.

Oh, great, thought our girl, *I can see the headlines now:*
Queen Crowned by Crackhead While Getting Moob-Lubed by Cow.
The dog dropped the stick and ran off at a tear
to join his pal licking grease from a tipped-over chair.

He/She kept squeezing, but it was doing no good,
especially fearing the whip of walking stick wood.
But that wood whip never came, and what came instead
made He/She turn 'round with surprise, shaking her head.

"You're doing it all wrong!" said the hairy-chest pimp.
"Make a hard fist and grab it, and don't be a wimp.
Jerk up, and hard, or it's the trachea knife.
Quick! My auntie was a nurse for half of her life!"

He/She didn't question this unexpected tip.
She wiped off the grease and readjusted her grip.
Then with all of her might, she jerked like a boy scout
and the next thing she knew—kack!—a wee bone flew out.

As the large man recovered, our He/She got up
and saw to her dismay she was covered in guck.
Lardo coughed a bit at the pimp and said, "T'anks, dude."
Then like nothing happened, he reached for more food.

The pimp leaned on his cane and gave He/She a squint.
"Now get going!" he growled, (and did he need a mint!)
"You've no more business here, so get moving along.
On these seven blocks and the next, you don't belong."

While He/She counted to ten, he spat on the walk,
a yellow jelly gob, like some kind of sick jock.
"There's no business," said He/She. "As I've said to you,
I'm only walking my dogs and just passing through.

"So, thank you for helping with your weird expertise.
You're the first pimple ever to teach me to squeeze."
Then, two leashes in hand, she turned to get away
from the sights and the smells of this psycho soirée.

Sadly, the pimp wasn't keen on what she'd said
and a few blows of the cane rained down on her head.
It took a minute or so to fend off the freak.
She broke two or three nails, but of that we won't speak.

They got 'round the corner. He/She just had to stop
outside the closed iron gates of some kind of junk shop.
"Well, that was the strangest thing I ever did see,"
said our girl, all gasted by flab. "And look at me!

"Top to tail, I've been smeared with fat, sweat and spurt.
And oh—ew! There's an old french fry stuck to my skirt!"
"Stop whining," said a pekepoo. "What about us?
There's something about dinner we need to discuss."

"And water!" said his twin. "After all that lickin',
everything tastes like regurgitated chicken."
Onward He/She ventured under the dim streetlights,
with ruined nails and makeup, her hair just a fright.

The first store they went in wouldn't let her pups stay
so after a quick piddle, they went on their way.
Progress was slow, her blistering heels were on fire
and god knows her poor toes felt wrapped in barbed wire.

After a while she was taking any excuse
to find some small place to sit and slip off her shoes.
Scuffed and a torture, she had to keep wearing them,
what with the needles and glass and—ugh—old man phlegm.

At last they found a food truck to buy a small snack,
not suspecting at all they'd be under attack.
For just when He/She reached into her treasured chest,
there jumped out a smug kid in a black leather vest.

"Must be nice to be rich," he smarmed, eyeing her cash,
his teeth all yellow under a wormy moustache.
Before she even clued in that she was his mark,
he grabbed all her money and ran off in the dark.

"Now what," snarked a poo, "are you going to do
to get him and I a drink and much-needed food?"
He/She's heart sank for a moment. "This is unreal!
Can it get any worse? This is far from ideal!"

After a few hard sighs, she went back to the truck
and returned with water in a sad paper cup.
"Careful! Try not to spill, puppies. That's all there is!
Oh, what I wouldn't give for a mango rum fizz!"

When the pekepups were done their paper cup lap,
one of them began crabbing and started a scrap.
"You had three licks more water and I hate your guts!"
"You shut up!" said the other. "Your breath smells like nuts!"

They started to snarl and attack with their teeth
and twisted up He/She in one another's leash.
Before our girl knew it, her shoe caught in a grate
and off came a heel like it was some kind of fate.

She scolded her doggies for a second or two
before galumphing on in her busted-ass shoe.
Up, down, up, down, just like her dogs jumping for cheese.
Sadly, no one was feeding her in a chemise.

Three blocks on, they seemed to enter a new town,
with streets lined with factories of red brick and brown.
Broken windows, slinking dogs, every car a wreck—
it all scared up the hairs on the back of her neck.

As she passed them, the hoods of gangs turned in the dark,
watching her like she was chum and they were all sharks.
One of them threw a bottle, which was quite indescrete
for her heart nearly landed right plop in the street.

As they went up a hill, He/She said, "What was that?
It sounded like a baby. Or was it a cat?
I just hate this place—I think it might hate itself.
At this moment I'd rather be anywhere else!"

Well, as luck would have it, her wish almost came true.
They reached the top of a hill where fresh breezes blew.
Then formerly orderly elegant He/She
raised her nose to the wind, and surprise, smelled salt sea!

Intermixed with the sea came that horrible stench
that made the walls of every orifice clench.
It was downhill from here—she could see the last street
and beyond it the water and rugged rock beach.

"It smells like food!" said a poo. "Remember that time
He/She had clams and we got the leftover slime?"
"Of course," said the other, "it was simply sublime.
And once she had lobster! I swear there was scads!
Just don't mention that time that she almost had crabs."

He/She hobbled down, or rather, up and down,
like a true Queen of Drag (both the verb and the noun).
The horrible aroma was far stronger here.
She was not even sure she could stand to be near!

They arrived at the street, which was quite busy with cars.
"It's to the right," said a poop, "and not very far."
Between the street and the beach was a tall chain-link fence
that blocked most of the view and upped the suspense.

After a little ways on, they crossed to a gate
only to find it locked and the hour too late.
The beach closed at nine and it was now well past that.
"We've come too far, my muttkins, for this to fall flat!"

He/She could see just inside, a distance away,
a small fire on the rocks, sparks blowing like spray.
But what was that figure hunched there like a lump?
Was it a rock? A cute buoy? Or some person's rump?

"Oh, lovely," said a poopeke, "now what do we do?"
"Yeah, do what and how?" added poopeke number two.
"I get your big quest; the stink is quite uncanny.
But come on! I'd rather be home in my jammies."

"I'm going to climb it," said He/She. "You two stay here.
I might fall, so really, you had better stand clear."
The pekes rolled their eyes and went to the curb and stood.
"I like a show," said one, "and this oughta be good."

Our He/She pried off what was left of her shoes,
her dainty feet like tartare, all red, raw and blue.
Parting her sticky toes so they'd fit in the fence,
she took in a breath before the real fun commenced.

Then up He/She went, and with each step gave a shriek,
thinking, *This hurts far worse than a bad waxing technique.*
She got right to the top with tears clouding her eyes,
forgetting heights like this gave her bad butterflies.

Try to be calm, she thought, *and try not to look down,
or your royalous self might end up on her crown.*
The wire on the top scratched the heck from her thighs,
but the bustier rips deserved some kind of prize.

She inched herself down, blinking little toe tears,
knowing once she got home, she'd have scar souvenirs.
When she reached the concrete, the world broke out in song.
And there were her pups, saying, "What took you so long?"

They'd got on their bellies and scooched underneath
and were now lounging on the rocks, picking their teeth.
"What are you eating?" asked He/She. "And what the hell?
Is that the source of our problem? That god-awful smell?"

"Couldn't tell ya," said pupdog numero uno.
"It goes down like a boxer, that is all I know."
Both mutts were eating some kind of wriggly ick.
"Ugh! Stop that!" said He/She. "You'll make yourselves sick!"

She tried to retrieve it, but both dogs ran away
gnawing their horrible find, to He/She's dismay.
The lump was still sitting with its back to the glow
of the fire's sparking embers, which blew to and fro.

And in that blowing, He/She could hardly get air.
It was obvious the stink was coming from there.
This was the kack's cradle, icky-poo's bassinet.
It was Death and Diarrhea, singing duet.

Bravely our He/She stepped off the pad of concrete
onto the slippy rocks with her sore little feet.
She balanced with care, using both hands and screams
and made her way close to where the reek was extreme.

"Excuse me," said He/She to the dark lumping thing,
feeling her lunch coming up as if on a string.
When she got no reply, He/She checked out the fire,
wishing she could trade her skirt for hazmat attire.

Laid out on the fiery coals was a great charred beast.
Goodness! She recoiled. *I'm glad that thing's deceased!*
There was a beak, tentacles and sharp, pointy fin.
It had big grabby crab claws and slick, scaly skin.

"Excuse me," she said again, approaching with care,
balancing on the rocks and trying not to swear.
She circled the lumping lump. "Hello," she said.
"You're not moving too much, so I hope you're not dead."

Then crouching down, she had a terrible surprise;
the smell over here made the tears leap to her eyes.
It wasn't the fish heap, her pups' tentacled banquet.
The reek was coming straight from under that blanket!

A third time she said, "Excuse me," tapping the lump,
which was suctioning her stomach just like a pump.
 "I've travelled quite far," she said, "looking for you.
I got all dressed up nice and my wee dogs did too.

"We walked a very long way, I got beat up twice
by these people who should have been—could have been—nice.
My toes are a total wreck, my fingernails worse,
and god knows my hair could use a registered nurse."

The lump just sat there, the same as when they arrived.
He/She wondered if it was even alive.
So she gave it a poke, and it turned its head slow,
like a very old person in stiff neck slow-mo.

He/She felt anger rise up—she'd come all this way!
The least they could do was not turn away!
"What is wrong with you? That smell is really severe.
Don't ignore me! I've suffered all the way here!"

But the lump it just sat there like a bacon-wrapped prune.
That's when He/She stopped yelling and changed up her tune.
"Oh, please don't ignore me. I'm so very tired.
Don't hate me. The stink's strong. And I'm really wired."

When the lump didn't move, He/She had to sit down,
her lower back sacked after her walk across town.
She didn't care about the reek, this hellish whiff.
Without rest it would be the last thing she sniffed.

A minute later, our He/She was fast asleep,
her dogs curled by her legs like little lost sheep.
They slept for an hour, making a sweet snoring noise,
then woke to what sounded like an old woman's voice.

"I've been sitting here since this morning," the voice said,
sounding creaky and croaky and really half-dead.
"I was born with this smell. It's a horrid disease—
a riotous reek like rot and old German cheese.

"I have lost my apartment, I can't get a job.
Wherever I travel there's a rude pointing mob.
I have hardly had a friend, and of course, no lover.
You're the first person to sleep beside me, ever."

By now He/She was sitting up and wide awake,
not just sore but with a great big hearty heartache.
"But why are you here? And what on earth's with the fish?
It's so weird, it looks like it crawled from the abyss."

After a deep cough, the lump croaked, "Oh, yes, well…
I've been banned from the beach, and that masks the smell.
I got all the dead things that washed up on the rocks.
It's all I could think of to keep away the cops."

"But why here?" asked He/She. "This is all quite bizarre."
And the lump said, "I have been living in my car
for the past nine months, and it's more than I can stand.
You seem so nice. I won't say what I had planned."

"What?" exclaimed He/She. "Were you going to kill yourself?"
"Well…" said the lump, "I was. But I might need your help.
It's not an easy matter to make yourself drown.
I'm hoping you can help me by holding me down."

He/She's mouth went agape. "That's out of the question!
Gals like me call that a serious transgression."
"That's okay," croaked the lump, "just, please, when you go,
don't call up the police or let anyone know.

"Oh, and here, take these keys, you can have my old car.
Thank you so much. It sounds like you came really far."
He/She took the lump's keys and struggled to her feet.
She could see an old beater parked off down the street.

"This is ridiculous!" said He/She. "You can't die!
There's got to be drugs! Clinics! At least you can try!"
But the lump shook its head. "I have tried all of that.
Deodorants, sprays, testing. I'm not some lab rat!

"Thanks so much for your concern, but before you go,
I'll die happy because of you. I just want you to know.
Now please leave. You're lovely; we could have been friends.
But it's my life, and I get to say how it ends."

Right then, the lump began throwing stones at our doll.
She had to move away fast and try not to fall.
What to do? He/She fretted, a distance away.
She couldn't simply drive home. She just had to stay!

So she sat on a rock and waited with her pups.
No one else seemed to care! She just had to step up!
The nearest street light was really not very near,
and if there was a moon out, it wasn't near here.

So she sat and sat, happy to have a nice rest,
though she had to admit she was completely stressed.
How did she end up here, after that great big hike,
playing fateful finger in that old lady's dike?

But our girl was not used to being up this late.
("Early to bed" she'd advise a really good date.)
She needed her sleep, and as the hours slipped by
the day's two curtains began to slip down her eyes.

She woke with a start with her pups curled in her lap.
Oh, goodness! thought He/She, *I didn't mean to nap!*
The cold tide had come in and was up 'round her toes.
It had drowned and extinguished the fish fire's glow.

Then she noticed something strange—or rather, not strange.
The air was quite clear. There was no stink for a change!
But the moment she noticed her heart almost stopped.
"Oh, no!" she said, standing, as both doggles dropped.

"What TF?" said her dogs, in a figure of speech
as He/She splash-hobbled across the swamped beach.
"Oh, no, no, no, no," a horrified He/She said.
"Please don't let that granny be all drowned and dead!"

She rushed through the water, stubbing every toe twice.
"I'm so sorry I slept, don't let her pay the price!"
As she searched the black waters, her pups barked like nuts,
"She's here! No, there! Come on! Quit being such a klutz!"

He/She scrambled frantically, at both walk and crawl,
her voice choked with emotion when she tried to call.
Then just as she thought, *I've lost her! I'm a disgrace!*
she tripped over something and fell flat on her face.

It was a lump in a blanket, more dead than alive.
"Oh, please!" cried out He/She, "You've got to survive!"
Then with the buns of Bonnie and the guns of Clyde
she lifted the lump out of the dark, drowning tide.

Aiming herself toward a big hole in the fence
(made clam-shaped by clammers, making symbolic sense),
she stumbled the lump over the toe-killing rocks,
out through the hole, and to the old car up the block.

He/She's two poogles followed, burping up squid,
both of them crying "Shotgun!" like two little kids.
She laid the lump in the back seat, which smelled like…yikes!
and once her mups were in, they screeched off in the night.

She knew quite well where the nearest hospital was,
as anyone who ever drank tequila does.
"Hurry up!" cried a pupapeke. "She's fighting for air!
Here, we'll lie on her chest—so don't say we don't care."

Six minutes later, with the pedal to the floor,
they arrived at the busy emergency door.
Her pups seemed fine, so with the lump in her arms,
she raced in through the doors and raised the alarm.

"Oh, help!" she yelled loudly. "Can someone help, please!
This poor person has nearly drowned in the sea!"
"Have a seat," said a nurse to our desperate doll.
"We'll help right away. Dr. Kenneth is on call."

Well, at this point our He/She nearly lost her mind
and tried very hard to keep calm and refined.
Thankfully for her, she knew this nice Dr. Ken.
He liked to play doctor at her house now and then.

As fast as they could, they wheeled away the reek,
for the intake nurse had lost the power to speak.
Dr. Kenny came out saying, "Well, look who it is!
Did someone have a bit too much mango rum fizz?

"Tell me everything, darling; let's sit over there.
Here, let me help, you look like you've had quite a scare."
Right then He/She broke down, holding onto his hand.
She was glad to have someone so nice understand.

She launched into the tale of her Jungle of Jools
and the driblets of stink landing plop in her pool.
Then there was all the bad luck on her noble quest
to locate the vile smell blowing in from the west.

Then just as she got to the old lump's suicide,
two sad-looking pekepoos raced in from outside.
Some intern followed them, saying, "Oh! There you are!
These dogs have to leave, and could you please move your car?"

"Go ahead," said Dr. Ken. "Don't worry at all.
See you in a minute. I'll be just down that hall."
He/She limped back to the car and had a big fight
with a big, wobbling sob before she was all right.

But a parking place close? There just wasn't any.
And the doc's minute quickly turned into twenty.
She left the pups inside with two windows cracked.
"We're good," they both said, "we have a car to ransack!

"This deep, fetid odor may not smell good to you,
but to us it's glorious Chanel No. 2."
Barefoot, exhausted, He/She returned to the ward
and sat for twelve horrid minutes, completely bored.

Finally and at last, when dear Dr. Ken called
she anxiously followed him down two different halls.
They ended up just outside this pale, greenish curtain—
a colour, thought He/She, which made sickness certain.

"Your friend," said the doctor, "is extremely unwell,
that's aside from the fact of that god-awful smell.
It may be pneumonia or a bad strep throat case.
Truth is, either way, he has a long road to face."

Right then He/She's head jerked in the most shockful way.
"Say who—what?" she blurted, blinking. "What did you say?"
"He'll be fine," said the doc; "give him ten days or so.
Then he'll be on his feet and you can take him home."

"Heh?" said our He/She, pushing the curtain aside.
But she was not quite prepared for what was inside.
The most angelic boy lay sleeping sweetly there,
about twenty, she guessed, with light golden hair.

"Is this the lump I brought in a short while ago?"
"Minus the blanket," said Doc Ken, "I'm afraid so.
It's understandable, your mistaking his voice.
Being so unwell, he has to croak to make noise."

Well, right then the last bit of He/She's mascara
won a free trip to the cheekbone riviera.
"Just bear in mind," said the doc, "I know it sounds bleak,
he'll be on suicide watch, the next couple weeks.

"I think it would be helpful—in fact, help a lot,
if you came by to visit, more often than not."
He/She could only nod at the doctor's advice.
Oh, hell, yes, she thought. He didn't have to ask twice.

"Now, my girl," said Doctor Ken, "I think what is best
is you should get yourself home and have a nice rest."
In a blur of exhaustion and happy relief,
He/She trudged down the hall, in complete disbelief.

What had just happened? Was this all really true?
Should she laugh or tear up after all she'd been through?
Look at me, she thought. *I'm half black and blue,
barefoot, hair destroyed, on my last shred of style.
But holy dear moly, was it ever worthwhile.*

With two limps and a grin she got to the front door
just as the morning's first light poured into the ward.
But the place was quite busy; you couldn't move fast,
and when she got to the doors, she had to squeeze past.

They were helping an unlucky guy and his bride
and neither looked up as they were carried inside.
He was an Ital young man, his crotch packed with ice,
and she…she wore a big ring and had been shot twice.

Thinking this was Miss Karma's last call of the night,
she got outside to discover it wasn't, quite.
What were they unloading a short distance away?
Aaahh…a great big fatty who'd arrived DOA.

She and her pups got home in the former lump's car,
glad to kiss this long night a final au revoir.
Toward six o'clock, she fell asleep in the bath
with fizzy mango rum in a very tall glass.

For the next two weeks she visited every day,
properly primped and dressed in her usual way.
She dabbed his forehead, snuck in all kinds of treats,
resisting the temptation to smooth out his sheets.

Then came the day when he was sufficiently well
to get out of both bed and the sickie hotel.
Our He/She felt happy. She was helping him dress,
thinking of special sponge baths while he convalesced.

"You know," said the lad, "I would have died without you.
I had both pneumonia and a bad case of flu.
For days I couldn't eat. I was out of my mind.
I just have to say thank you for being so kind."

And right then the sweet boy kissed her on the cheek,
leaving there a spot of semi-permanent reek.
Though He/She couldn't help but turn six shades of red,
all of a sudden, her heart was stricken with dread.

"You know," he continued, "nothing can be compared
to how I feel about you. I thought no one cared.
Honestly, I didn't think I was into men,
but I've fallen in love with our good Doctor Ken."

He/She had had visions of summer afternoons
with drinks in the pool till they were shrivelled like prunes.
What had her pups said this morning as she picked out a skirt?
"If you keep talking like that you're going to get hurt."

The boy sighed and continued. "Please understand.
He's taking me to a clinic in Amsterdam.
After that, he has promised me he'll pay for school
and get me an apartment that has its own pool!"

He/She wished him well, she even patted his hair.
Twelve seconds later, she got the fuck outta there.
She spent a total of no time shaking her head
at this kid she had saved from ending up dead.

She had a party to plan. Décor to devise.
She could mail invitations with spangles inside.
There would be hors d'oeuvres and cocktails, all of that stuff.
"I can't wait to call up all my pals to discuss."

But when she arrived home and her pups heard the tale,
they rolled their eyes, then nearly barked themselves pale.
"Aren't you angry deep down? Is this just a façade?
Surely there's at least one vengeful bone in your bod.

"Come on. Normal people throw some dishes and pout.
And what the heck's all this party planning about?"
He/She calmly smiled and poured herself a nice drink.
"Well, my darling pupakins, it's not what you think.

"I'm not going to forget or try to forgive.
I don't even care about live and let live.
Clichés are all boring. Life is like a fondue:
The best fruit ain't the best till it's been through some goo."

Then she sashayed out to her Jungle of Jools
to fashion her party in the Pool of the Cool.
There she splashed… in a vintage two-piece pastel,
He/She the Elegant, at last free of that smell.